REACHING FOR VENUS

MAIJA BARNETT

WEST 44 BOOKS™

**Please visit our website, www.west44books.com.
For a free color catalog of all our high-quality books, call toll free 1-800-398-2504.**

Cataloging-in-Publication Data
Names: Barnett, Maija.
Title: Reaching for Venus / Maija Barnett.
Description: Buffalo, NY : West 44, 2025. | Series: West 44 YA verse
Identifiers: ISBN 9781978597334 (pbk.) | ISBN 9781978597327 (library bound) | ISBN 9781978597341 (ebook)
Subjects: LCSH: Sisters--Juvenile fiction. | Space colonies--Juvenile fiction. | Venus (Planet)--Juvenile fiction.
Classification: LCC PZ7.1.B376 Re 2025 | DDC [F]--dc23

First Edition

Published in 2025 by
Enslow Publishing LLC
2544 Clinton Street
Buffalo, New York 14224

Editor: Caitie McAneney
Designer: Tanya Dellaccio Keeney

Photo Credits: Cover Vezdehod/Shutterstock.com; interior background nednapa/Shutterstock.com.

Printed in the United States of America

CPSIA compliance information: Batch #CS25W44: For further information contact Enslow Publishing LLC at 1-800-398-2504.

For my sister, Ariel

WALKING HOME

I taste the sky—
toxic and gray.

Smothering my lungs.
Making them burn.

My sister Rachel
is at my side.

"You're okay, Lee-Lee,"
she whispers.

"Look, we're
almost there."

I glance back at the
Forgotten City—

empty as a
broken shell.

Rachel holds our basket
of finds.

Some canning jars,
in their
original packaging.

An unopened
bottle of
wine.

Things we can sell at
The Stalls.

So we can pay
for food
and heat—

and medicine for
my lungs.

"Breathe," says Rachel,
her long, black hair
slipping
from its
heavy bun.

I tuck a strand
behind her ear
and think of how
it's just like
mine.

"I'm okay,"
I wheeze.

But that's
a lie.

My lungs are
screaming.

My throat is
raw.

The air I'm getting
isn't
enough.

I search my pockets
for my
inhaler.

But then I remember
the cartridge
ran
  out.

"We'll get one tomorrow,"
Rachel says.
"Angus will
hook us up."

I nod and focus on
the view.

Our cottage,
tucked into
     the hillside.

Dad built it from
"found material."

(Which means
other people's junk.)

I picture Dad
the year he died.
He had asthma
just like me.

Almost there, I think.
Focus, Leah.

I reach for my
sister's
     hand.

Trying to forget
how it hurts
     to breathe.

US

Some people laugh
at our names.

Straight from a book
no one owns
anymore.

It's been so long,
only the Olds
remember.

The pairing of Rachel
and her sister, Leah.

The pairing of
my sister
and me.

We're a year apart,
but we look
like twins.

At least that's what
everyone says.

Except we're different in an
important way.

I'm one year older and
100 years
weaker.

My asthma steals
everything.

Our money.

My breath.

My life someday, too.

After Dad died,
Mom was close
behind.

Now it's just
Rachel and me.

Rachel's the boss,
even though she's the
little sister.

Rachel is the one
who keeps us
alive.

RACHEL'S CHANCE

There's something
we don't
talk about.

A ticket out.
Just for one.

I'll give you a hint—
It takes four months
to get there.

Then you live inside
a yellow
sky.

About 31 miles
above
the planet's
scorched surface.

Beautiful Venus,
with her floating city.

Her gift of life
trapped
in the stars.

16

Here, 16 is an
important number.

It's the age they decide
if you can
go.

"They" is Terra,
the government
that gives us
nothing.

Except for
one chance,

when you turn
16.

Only 50 boys
and 50 girls,

from all across our
dying Earth.

It's a contest,
but only the healthy
can enter.

That means
Rachel.

It doesn't mean
me.

But you need
skills, too.

And Rachel
has them.

She can grow flowers
in a pinch
          of soil.

Coax scarlet
tomatoes

from dried-up
vines.

On December 31st,
they make their
                    decision.

We're on the
edge now.

It's almost
here.

Every breath
takes us
a little bit
          closer.

Every breath
fills
   my heart
          with fear.

HISTORY

This wasn't always
how it was.

Years ago, we were a
global society.

The Forgotten City was
Worcester, Massachusetts.

One tiny piece
of the
          USA.

There were
other states,
and countries, too.

Instead of just Terra
for everyone.

I've seen photos
in books
buried in the library.

Crumbling in
the center
          of town.

(That building scares me,
but Rachel likes to go.

I keep lookout,
just in case.)

Everything changed,
when the seas
rose.

And the air grew
hard to breathe.

But our forefathers
had a plan.

A mission to Mars,
and Venus, too.

They wanted to build
two new
homes.

Just in case
one
didn't
work out.

The Mars mission
failed.

That colony
split.

Like the apples we pluck
from the dusty roadside.

Their mealy insides
full of
worms.

So Mars was
lost.

The city
burned

by an angry faction
who destroyed
everything.

All that was left
was the
Floating City.

That goddess who whispers
in our deepest dreams.

Her yellow clouds—
a paradise.

ORPHANS

Mom and Dad
taught us
all they could.

Once they realized
what was
coming.

Once they knew
how little time
they had
left.

They built
a greenhouse
with raised
garden beds.
To stop the rains
from flooding
our crops.

An irrigation system
from a bale of
twisted-up tubing.

(Rachel's friend Angus
scored that for us.

And sold it
to Rachel
for less than it was
worth.)

"Better than diamonds!"
Dad had joked.

Because diamonds
don't mean
anything here.

We set it up,
while Mom and Dad
stayed
in bed,
Instructing us
on what to do.

Rachel calls
our system
Mom and Dad's
gift.
Even though
they're not
with us,
their handiwork is.

Every time we slice
into a
bleeding
tomato.
Or trade
fresh greens
at The Stalls.
Mom's voice
whispers
in my ear.

A ghost of the promise
she made me
make.

After Dad
was gone.

THE PROMISE

Rain pounded our
metal roof.

Making it
hard
to hear.

Rachel was in the
greenhouse
tending plants.

I was inside
tending
someone else.

Deathwatch, I thought,
though we didn't
call it that.

We just said Mom
was resting.

Waiting for when
she'd meet up with
Dad.

I was adjusting her blanket
when she grabbed my arm.

"Leah," she wheezed.
Her voice a kettle's
hiss.

"If Rachel's chosen,
make her go.

She's the only chance
this family has."

"Promise," said Mom,
fingers hot on my wrist.

Her dark eyes
full of
    fear.

"I promise," I whispered,
looking away.

Trying my best
to swallow
    the lie.

ANGUS LEE

Angus Lee
loves
my sister.

At first,
I was blind.
I just thought
they were friends.

That he was our
connection
at The Stalls.
With his makeshift
hearing aids
and sick parents
at home.

(Angus couldn't
apply to the
Floating City.
His congenital hearing loss
meant
he was out.)

Angus has a lot
to worry about.
But he always
has time
for Rachel and me.

Well, mostly Rachel,
if I'm being
          honest.

But he sells me
inhaler cartridges
for cheaper
then he
should.

And his dark eyes
sparkle
whenever Rachel's
around.

"What's with you
and Angus?"
I once asked,
when we were
in the greenhouse,
weeding.

"Nothing," scoffed Rachel,
trying not
to smile.

"He likes *you*," she joked.
"You're the same age,
you know."

"Funny," I said,
knowing the
truth.

Then I pictured
Angus's kind
eyes.

And hoped
he'd be enough
to make
Rachel stay.

WHAT RACHEL SAYS

I run down
the path
to meet her.
Her hair is
flecked
in snow.

"How was it?"
I puff.
My breath almost
gone.

Rachel grabs my wrists
and
          grins.

Her bright eyes
full of
          hope.

She tells me
she found
the testing site.

It was a day's walk,
due west.

Just like they'd said
on the TV wall
that stares down
from The Stalls
like a watchful eye.

But she made it,
and on her birthday.

December 22nd—
the only day
she's
          eligible.

"The blood work
went fine,"
          Rachel says.

"They only took
three vials."

I picture
liquid darkness
streaming
from her.

A masked face,
cold as the
              sea.

"Lee-Lee," she says,
"I think I passed.
The physical was easy.
And the MRI, too.
The written work
was a little
tough,
but I did
          okay."

Her eyes
glitter
with a secret.

I wish I knew
what it was.

WAITING

It's December 31st.
And Rachel's
quiet.
She doesn't want
to go to The Stalls.

My body pulses with
anticipation.
I ache to watch the
TV screens.
Wait for Terra's
announcement.

But Rachel says
we've got stuff
to do.
An irrigation line
froze
last night.

(The greenhouse work is
never-ending.)

"Besides," says Rachel,
faking a smile,
"we'll find out
either way."

I close my eyes
and do what she asks.
While trying to ignore
my shaking
hands.

FINDING OUT

I'm thinning
lettuce
when I hear him.

It's Angus,
calling
my sister's name.

"Rachel!" he cries,
his voice rough.

I can tell he
ran
all the way from
The Stalls.

I fumble for the
greenhouse door.

And then
I'm outside,
watching them.

Angus's arms are
wrapped
around my sister.

Rachel has
started to cry.

"Rachel?" I say.

Heat rushes
through me.

She turns her head
and says,
          "We're safe."

GO!

We're running
toward
the Forgotten City.

Panic pulses
through
my veins.

Moments ago, I was
watching
        Rachel.

Who was
laughing and sobbing
in Angus's arms.

Then Angus's
hand
was on my
        back.

While Rachel
rushed
into the house.

And came out with a
pack
slung over
        her shoulder.

"Let's go," she hissed.
"We need
        to hurry!

Terra's guards
will expect you
at intake
          soon.

And we still have to
work
everything out."

"Work what out?"
I asked.

But Angus
motioned for
silence.

As if he thought
someone
might be
          listening
                    in.

So now we're
sprinting
down the path.

My lungs
burn,

but Rachel
pushes me
          forward.

Into the city
I
   fear.

HIDEAWAY

We're somewhere off
Highland Street.

Inside a tavern
from the
past.

Rachel hauls me
through a
doorless
doorway.

And into a room of
broken glass.

Thick dust
coats
everything.

But the bar
still
stands.

And Angus is
behind it.

Clawing at something
on the floor.

"Where are we?"
I gasp.

Taking a pull
from my
inhaler.

Rachel presses
a finger
to her lips.
Then motions me
behind the bar.

Where Angus
reveals
a hidden staircase.

I stare at the hole
at my feet.

Its musty darkness
whispers,
"Come."

ANGUS'S STASH

We huddle around
the single candle
that Rachel pulled
from her pack.

I scan
the cellar's walls.

There are bits of
machinery.
A crate of
canned food.

I spy a box of
ammunition.
And a stack of
first aid kits.

Rachel ignores our strange
surroundings.

Her gaze
locked on Angus, instead.

"Well," says Angus,
clearing his throat.

Shadows slip across
his face.
But his eyes stay
kind.

"Welcome to my
black market stash, Leah.
Now we'll explain
the plan."

THE PLAN

"You're taking
the *Egress*
in my place,"
says Rachel.

Once you get to the
Floating City,
you'll finally be
safe."

My eyes grow
wide.

"I can't," I say.

"Well, you're going,"
Angus replies.

Then their voices
are a
swollen
stream.

Catching me
in its
path.

WHAT RACHEL DID

Rachel filled out the
paperwork
        for me.

Wore special fingertips
that Angus made
on a
borrowed
        3D printer.

"Cost me a box
of bullets,"
        he says.

The prints on the
fingertips
were mine.

(Stolen
while I slept.)

"But my asthma,"
I say when Rachel's
                        done.

"We researched," says Angus.
"Talked to healers,
                        too.
Once you're out of this air,
you'll be
        fine."

"Just don't let them run
any tests," adds Rachel.

"Your lungs are
permanently
scarred.

Also, I'm blood type O
and you're A,"
she adds.

"Don't EVER let them
find that
out."

GOING

I'm picked up
at The Stalls.

Angus waits
with me.

Rachel
stays home.

(We couldn't risk
anyone
figuring things out.)

I stare at the guards
from the Floating City.

Armed with
guns.

Their uniforms
crisp.

Stern faces—
full of
health.

Angus gives
my hand
a squeeze.

I pretend to be
Rachel,
and hug him
goodbye.

Then I make myself
walk.

Past the hungry
faces.

The wind-tattered
tents.

Merchants selling
their wares.

Part of me aches to
refuse
this gift.

But Rachel
made the choice
for both
of us.

Her love for
Angus.

Her love
for me.

I feel it deep
inside my
chest.

Its bitter
strands

pull
tight.

DR. BREEN, JANUARY 1

"I remember you,"
the doctor
says.

I want to
laugh.

(Something I do
when I'm
nervous.)

But I
grit my teeth
instead.

All the while,
her
blue eyes
take me in.

She looks
about 40,

which is old
for Earth.

(My parents died
younger than
that.)

She's blonde and pretty,
except for her
smile.

Which stretches
over her face
in a twisted
line.

Don't trust her,
I think,

growing
cold.

I'm in the
medical tent
for my final
check-in.

The Venusian guards just
brought me in.

We rode a
helicopter
to get here.

(I've only seen
those
in
books!)

Dr. Breen presses
my fingers
into a
machine.

Then waves a
tan wand
across my
brow.

"We assessed you
two weeks ago,"
she says.
"That means you're
all set."

Angus was right, I think,
blinking back
tears
of relief.

*They're not going to do
a full health
check.*

I force myself
off the
examination
table.

And out into
Earth's
fading light.

Don't cough,
I think.

*You'll give yourself
away.*

A launchpad
stands
in front of me.

The silver *Egress*
silently waits.

I touch the part of my
backpack
that holds my
                    inhaler.

A secret pocket
I have to pray no one
                              sees.

"Soon I won't need you,"
I whisper
to the
          hidden hunk of
          plastic.

"Soon I'll be
someone
          else."

BLASTOFF!

I have my own cabin—
metallic and cold.

This ship could hold
600
        souls.

But there are only
100
rescued souls here.

(Plus the crew, so make that
130.)

*Why won't they save
anyone else?*

I peer out the window
as we leave Earth
behind.

Hold my breath
when we roar
into
        blackness.

And picture
my sister's
        smile.

FOUR LONG MONTHS

I try to keep
                    to myself.

Better than to
slip up and
          forget.

Each morning I whisper,
"Remember,
          you're Rachel."

Then I take a
deep drag from my
inhaler.

Even though I'm
not sure
          I need it
                    anymore.

We're supposed to exercise
an hour a day.

To keep our muscles
strong
and ready
for work.

So far, all I've done
is walk.

Nobody's said
                    anything.

SPACE FOOD

I sit
alone
in the cafeteria.

Before my daily,
inhaler-free
walk.

Outside,
stars glare
at my oatmeal.

Their cold eyes
watching
my glass
        of juice.

Orange is what
the cook said
it was.

As foreign to me as
space
        itself.

GHOST ME

The other 99 seem to have
got it.
I'm not here to make
friends.

But to be
a ghost
floating through
metallic
hallways.

Pale lights
skimming my
skin.

Yesterday,
I got a message
from Rachel.
It came in
on my
solar cell phone.

(They gave each of us
one
when we
boarded.

As a way to
communicate
and track us, too.)

Rachel's words
rang
in our
secret
code.

The one we
made up
when we were
small.

(Angus insisted
we use it
once I was
                    gone.
He said
it'd be tricky
for Terra's tech
                         to pick up.)

"Stay strong,"
said the
          message.

I wish
          I could.

My asthma's gone,
but a knot has formed.
It's in my throat
all the time.

Who are you?
I think,
peering
into the mirror.

Instead of Rachel,
all I see
          is me.

LEARNING

I spend all my time
in the ship's
library.

Learning about
my new
home.

The Floating City holds
around
100,000 people.

Its 150 platforms
are encased in
clear domes.

There's breathable air in the domes—
a mix of
nitrogen and oxygen.

The platforms float in Venus's
carbon-dioxide-
filled
sky.

They're miles above
the planet's
surface.

Where the
atmospheric pressure
is just like
Earth's.

Only not really
like Earth
    at all.

On Venus,
I won't have
my sister's
    smile.

Or the greenhouse we built
with our own
    hands.

It's a world full of strangeness
that slips
through the
    clouds.

Large propellers sit
at the base of
    each platform.

So the city can
follow the
    sunlight.

(It must, in order
to keep all that
solar energy
        flowing.)

And don't forget the
special polymer!

That clear,
plastic-like
    coating

(that's not plastic
at all).

It covers every part of the
Floating City.

Protecting our world from
acid rain.

ARRIVAL

Four long months
and we're
here.

Lyn, one of the
other
rescued—

the only one
I've really
spoken to

—waves from across
the room.

We're waiting
in the heart of
the *Egress.*

An open space
filled with
seats.

A screen slides
down
from the
ceiling.

And a picture of the
Floating City
appears.

Then the scene
switches

to a man
in a neat, blue
suit.

He's in an
office
made of
glass.

The city
bubbles out
behind him.

Its domes
sparkling
like jewels.

"Welcome,"
he says.

"I'm Captain Richard Jarvis,
head of our
settlement.

And beside
me,"

the camera pans
left,

"is my top security officer,
Lieutenant Anders Black."

Both men stare
at the screen.

I wonder why
they didn't meet us
in person?

Why are we
still on
the ship?

Captain Jarvis
looks
about 50.

His dark hair
laced
with gray.

The man beside him
is decades
younger.

With ghostlike skin
and wormy
lips

that make me
want to
look
away.

"In a moment, you'll begin
new lives,"
Jarvis says.

"Some will work on Sanitas,
our medical
platforms.

Others on Ingenium,
where we
construct
new domes.

And maintain the
oxygen
converters

that turn carbon dioxide
into breathable air.

A few will go to
Viridis,
our agricultural
platforms.

Where we grow
the food
that sustains
us all.

"Now," Jarvis continues.
His face is
hard.

"You're about to
be given
your assignments.

Just remember,
as you
complete
each task,

always follow
the city's
code.

Lieutenant Black
will now
explain."

RULES

Lieutenant Black
blinks his
watery eyes.

A pale tongue
darts
between
his lips.

"No lying," he booms.
(My heart
shudders.)

"No stealing.

No murder.

No having children
without state
permission."

He looks like
he's about to
smile.

"Know that
punishments are dealt out
quickly and severely.

Our trusted council will decide
your fate.

Most are sent
back to
Earth," says Black.

"But sometimes, if a crime
is severe . . ."

He's grinning now.

My stomach
knots.

A video starts
to play.

There's a man
standing
at the door of a
helium blimp.

The type that taxis
workers
between the city's
platforms.

A soldier rips away
the man's
oxygen mask.

And shoves him
into
the yellow
sky.

The screen
goes
dark.

At first
there's
silence.

Then people
speak
in panicked
whispers.

A few
start to
cry.

Finally, a voice
bleeds
through the walls.

Telling us
to listen
for our
assignments.

Most, including Lyn,
go to Sanitas,
the health
platforms.

The rest to Ingenium,
the building crew.

When the voice says
Viridis,
only one name
is called.

Rachel Silverton.

I scan the crowd
for my
sister.

But then I
remember.

The voice means
me.

VENUS

After boarding
one of the
floating
taxis,

I peer down
at the
city
below.

Sunlight glints
off
domed
platforms,

stretching out
across the
sky.

The air around us
glows
gold.

"We did it,
Rachel,"
I whisper to
no one.

But I can
feel
my sister's
presence.

Her warm hand
tight
in mine.

VIRIDIS

I know I'm in
Viridis
before we land.

My chest
        tightens
when I see all that
green.

Bright leaves
pressed against
        glistening domes.

Giant
terrariums.

Waiting to be
            explored.

MEETING ROSE

The floating taxi
puffs
through an air lock,
and we're finally
inside.

The flight was just
the pilot
          and me.

We didn't talk.
But now I wish
we had.

"Viridis," he calls,
          grinning hard.

His warm eyes say,
Welcome home.

He opens
the hatch,
and I step onto
a platform.

High above
the tree-lined
                    streets.

Guardrails block
me from
          falling.

Which is good
because

I can hardly
        breathe.
And this time
I can't
        blame it on
        my asthma.

But on the
emerald world
below.

"Rachel?"
says a girl,

stepping
        forward.

Bright red curls
gush down
        her back.

Her eyes
are the color of
summer grass.

"I'm Rose Palmer," she says,
reaching out
        her hand.

I take it
and stare at her
fairy face.

My heart
beating
        so loudly,

I swear
        she can hear.

VIRIDIS HAS . . .

Eight large platforms.
Each several miles
wide.

There's a dormitory on the
Primis platform.

Rose says that *primis*
is Latin for
"first."

(That dead language used
before even the
Olds
were young.)

My first day
is a blur
of green.

I feel myself
soaking in
everything.

My new room is
12 stories up.

It's on the
same floor
as Rose's.

There's just a
small
bed.

A desk and a
chair.

A shared
bathroom
down the hall.

Rose says
we bathe
twice a week.

We go in
shifts.

And we're not
to waste
water.

It's recycled
and there's
never enough.

"We mostly sponge bathe,"
says Rose.

"And keep our hair
short."

"Yours isn't," I say,
about to reach
for a
curl.

But then I
remember.

We've only
just
met.

So I grip
the side of my shirt
instead.

"No," she says.
touching her hair.

"I like it
this way.

It reminds me
of home."

For a moment,
her sparkle
disappears.

And a shadow
of sadness

slips behind
her eyes.

But she
blinks it
away

and leads me
to the window.

Showing me
all there is
to see.

While I decide
to keep
my hair long,
too.

THE VIEW

My room may be
plain.

But the view is
definitely
not.

Rose points
everything out.

The floating taxi stand
that you ride
a glass elevator
to get to.

The parks
sprouting
everywhere.

In Primis,
the plants grow
wild and fierce.

Rose says
Viridis's
other platforms
are more
orderly.

There are the
cornfields,
which I'll see
soon.

The veggie
platforms.

And the ones
for fruit.

"We use everything
we grow,"
        says Rose.

Her voice
brimming
        with pride.

I open my closet,
but nothing's there.

"We'll go to the laundry later,"
Rose laughs.

"But first, let's get you
something
        to eat."

CIBUS CAFE

"Cibus?" I ask.
Once we're seated.

Rose says it's a
fancy word
for food.

"Latin?" I guess.
She nods.

We're in a large,
one-story
building.

Brimming with
potted
          plants.

At the center sit
several
long, silver carts.

Each holding trays
of food.

"Salad bar," is what
Rose calls it.

I've never seen
so much food
in my life!

"Everyone on Viridis
eats here," Rose says.

"It's open
all day
long."

"No meat?" I ask
eyeing the
trays.

Bursting with greens
and
fruit.

My father's face
blooms
before me.

I remember the rabbits
he used to
bring
home.

Their soft ears
tucked
into his belt.

I liked their meat,
but their eyes
made me
sad.

Shiny and dark and
so much
like mine.

"Not here," says Rose,
nodding as a group
walks by.

No one stops to say
hello.

"You see," says Rose,
green eyes bright,
"animal products take
too much
space.

The Floating City is
mostly vegetarian."

"Mostly?" I ask.

"Well,"
Rachel smiles.

"We do have a platform
that farms
grubs.

The cooks
churn them up
and add them
for protein."

I can tell
she's waiting
for a
reaction.

But I just
smile.

"Back home," I say,
"we eat those,
too."

ROSE

While we eat,
Rose tells me about
her life.

She left Earth
last year,
when she turned 16.

A talented gardener
with a knack
for math.

She spends
half her time
on Acumen,
the education platform.

And the other
on Viridis,
tending
plants.

"When I was selected,"
she whispers,
leaning in,
"I told my mum
I didn't want to
go."

A bright piece
of lettuce
forgotten
on her
fork.

"But she said, 'Rose,
we have
five kids
        to care for.

I need at least
one
to be
        safe.'

I barely hear from them now,"
Rose says.

She lets out
a sigh.

And glances
        away.

When she
looks back,

I can tell
she's holding back
tears.

"Terra's internet cafes
cost
too much," she says.

"I told them
to buy
food
    instead."

"What are you studying
on Acumen?"
        I ask.

I want off the topic
of family
fast.

"Math," says Rose,
blinking hard.
Her green eyes
pull me
in.
"Plants and math
are safe,"
she says.

"They're honest in
every way.
It's people you have to
worry about.
The way they try and
scam you
at the market.
Break into your home
when you've got
nothing to steal.
Even your family
could be
lying."

Rose stops herself
and looks
away.

As if struggling
to keep something
locked
inside.

LAUNDRY

Everyone on Viridis
wears
tan jumpsuits

brimming with
        pockets.

("For tools,"
Rose laughs
when I ask why.)

Rose says it's all
blue and orange
        on Acumen.

"Thinking colors,"
she tells
        me.

We visit the laundry
after we eat.

And I get some
jumpsuits
of my
        own.

We're heading back to my room
when I
realize
        something.

Rose was
assigned
        to me.

What happens
when
she's done?

Will we even
talk
anymore?

She said she likes
plants
more than people.

What if she doesn't
really
like me?

My sister's face
flashes
before
me.

We might
look
the same.

But inside,
we're
not.

Rachel's
heart is
completely
selfless.

She never
once
thought about
leaving me.

Even now,
when she's
34 million miles
away.

I hear her
voice
inside my
head.

"You can do this,
Lee-Lee,"
she whispers.

"You can build a
brand
new
life."

FIRST NIGHT ALONE

Another meal
at the Cibus Cafe.

(Where I think
my burger
was made from
grubs.)

Then we head back
to the
        dorm.

Rose says it gets
dark
at 8:00 p.m.

The Floating City
follows Venus's
        sunshine.

(Because of the
amount
of energy
the solar panels
        need to make.)

That means it's never
actually
        night.

So at 8:00 p.m.,
the domes
        go black.

And our world
falls
        asleep.

I say goodnight
to Rose

and lie
        in bed.

Above me,
beyond the
        darkened dome,

clouds float through
the toxic
        sky.

I think of
Rachel and Angus,

who got me
here.

And feel them
smiling
in my
        mind.

HENRY PALMER

Rose wakes me at
6:00 a.m.

The dome
is clear,

and sunshine
          beams in.

After breakfast,
we ride the glass elevator
to the taxi
                    platform.

Rose laughs
          when we
                    climb aboard.

"Hey, cuz!" she cries
to the pilot—

a tall, muscular boy,
about 18.

Round cheeks
frame
          his grin.

But his hair
and eyes
are just like
               Rose's.

"Rosy!" he laughs,
pinching her cheek.

"Little cousin, I see
you've finally
made a
friend!"

"This is Rachel,"
says Rose,
rolling her
eyes.

"She just
got here
yesterday.

Rachel, meet Henry,
my favorite cousin
on Venus."

Henry
laughs.

"She says that
because
I'm the only
one!"

Then he tells us
to sit.
We're ready
for takeoff.

I stare in wonder
as Henry guides our
small blimp
through
the air lock
and into the
Venusian
sky.

THE TRIP

We're heading to
Platform Eight.

One of Viridis's
vegetable fields.

As we go, Henry
plays
tour guide.

His gestures and
voices
make me
smile.

"And over there," says Henry,
pointing to a large
gray box
sitting on a platform's
rim.

"That's one of the
converters they use
to suck
carbon dioxide
from Venus's
atmosphere.

And turn it into
breathable air."

"What about water?"
I ask.

Henry's eyes
bulge.

"Oh come on, Rachel,"
he says.
"You *really* don't
know?"

I shake
　　　　my head,

"Oh, Henry,"
　　　　　Rose sighs.

"I doubt Rachel
ever dreamed of
　　　　mining asteroids
　　　　　　　　for water
when she was
a little girl."

She turns to me
and tugs
　　　　my hair.

Something
inside
my chest
　　　　goes hot.

"That's all Henry's
ever wanted
　　　　to do," says Rose.

"If you'd only scored
higher
　　　　on your exams," she jokes.

"Though
I'm glad
　　　　you didn't.

Then I'd
never
see you."

Henry laughs.
"I'm here
to please.
Now stop your
chatting.
We're about to
land."

He guides us into
another
air lock.

Like a dancer
gliding
through empty
space.

"He's a great pilot,"
Rose whispers,
grabbing
my hand.

I nod as
my heart
becomes
a flower.

Opening for an
orange
sun.

FLORA AND THE TENDERS

"Flora Caper," says the woman,
holding out her hand.

Her brown eyes are
warm.

"How lovely to meet
a new tender," she says.

"New tender?"
I ask.

Rose
smiles.

We're standing
in the middle of
Platform Eight.

Around us bloom
rows of
squash.

And beyond that
tomato plants
stretch
high.

Flora laughs and adjusts
her many
braids.

Piled in a loose
bun.

Her skin is the color
of rich
earth.

"Tender means gardener,"
she says.

"But a gardener with
gentle
hands.

We tenders
know how
to help
plants grow.

I'll be your mentor,
like I am
for Rose."

She nods
at Rose,

who's standing
beside me.

Her green eyes
match
the vibrant
fields.

"Now, my tenders."
Flora smiles.

"Let's begin!"

WORK

My days begin to
bleed
together.

There are meals with
Rose
every night.

(Though I've met
several others
on Viridis,

I haven't
grown close
with anyone
else.)

On the days Rose works on
Viridis,
we take a taxi
together.

Sometimes
it's Henry's.

Sometimes,
not.

But when she's on
Acumen,

I travel
alone.

I've proven myself
a resourceful
gardener.

Keeping up with
the others
in the
fields.

But the greenhouse
is my favorite.

Mostly because
it reminds me of
home.

When my hands
dig deep in
cool soil,

I wonder if Rachel
is doing
the same.

FLORA

I've come
to love
my mentor,
Flora.

She works with all of
Viridis's
new recruits.

On Viridis,
the population
is kept
under control.

Only 100
pregnancies
are allowed
each year.

It's a lottery that
no one
dares
cheat.

(We all know
what
the punishment is.)

Flora and her partner, Tor,
donated their slot
to one of the
rescued.

So they
could save
a child of
Earth.

In return,
they get to
mentor.

"Besides,"
Flora tells me
while weeding
sunflower beds,
"plants are my children.

I sow their
seeds.

Raise them in the
nursery.

Then watch them
feed
everyone."

(Sunflower oil is used
for so much
here.)

"That means
we're eating
your babies," I say.

Flora's gentle
laughter

reminds me
I've found
my home.

LIFE IS . . .

Morning texts from Flora,
telling me where to go.

Mostly, I'm assigned to the
greenhouse.

Where the seedlings
make me smile.

After work, Rose and I
eat at the
Cibus Cafe.

Then we
visit the park.

While we walk,
Rose explains
what she's studying.

I talk
about my day.

At night, I lie in bed
and listen.

As Venus's rhythms
pulse through my veins.

Reminding me of all
I've been given.

Warning me
not to throw it
away.

INVITATION

I've been on Viridis
about a
month.

Dining with Rose
every day.

Learning from
Flora.

Exploring the
fields.

My asthma has
disappeared.

Today, it's the end
of my shift.

And I'm burying
my inhalers
beneath the greenhouse's
outer edge.

Like a trusted
friend
who's gone
to rest.

Or a forbidden
treasure
I might someday
need.

Whatever it is,
it's a place no one
will look.

At least, I seriously
hope
        they won't.

I glance up
and see
        Rose
walking toward me.

"Hi, Rach!" she chirps.
"I was hoping I'd
find
        you!"

She's wearing her
blue and orange
Acumen
        uniform.

And she glows
like a flower
in the yellow light.

"Henry says that
if you hurry,
he'll take us to
                The Ark."

"The Ark?" I parrot,
sweat prickling
my
    spine.

I'm afraid she going to
ask
what I'm
doing.

Why I'm digging
outside
the
greenhouse.
Instead of where
the plants
actually grow.

But Rose just
grins.

"You know, The Ark's
far away," she says.

"So it's hard
to visit.

And it's really something
you should
see!"

WITH HENRY

Henry smiles
when I climb
into
        his taxi.

"Ray-Ray!" he cries.

I catch
my breath.

Why is he
using
my pet name
for my
        sister?

For a moment,
something inside me
        twists.

But then Rose is
beside me.

And we're
                off.

Out to
the city's
distant rim.

"To the animals!"
hoots Henry.
        "Two by two!"

"You look confused,
Rachel."
Rose laughs.

I'm not.
But I still
        pretend.

There's so much of myself
I've hidden
        away.

It feels safer to become
someone new.

Safer than to mess up
and show
who I really am.

But I remember
this story.

It's one Dad
used to tell.

Taken from the book
where he got
        our names.

It's about a terrible
flood.

And some guy
named Noah.

Who kept
the animals
            alive.

He took
two of each kind.

And put them
in a boat.

Dad said that's
kind of what
Terra is doing.

Building an ark
out in space.

Trying to save
a few of us.

So life can
still
          go on.

THE ARK

"Back when they realized
Earth was dying," says Rose.

"The founders decided to
rescue animals.

They took a male and
a female of each
kind.

And built a platform
just for
them."

Rose continues on
about Africa's
scorched
savannas.

And how so many
creatures
were going
extinct.

All I can
picture
is my mother's
face.

Her ragged
cough

as she made me
promise.

To save
my sister.

Not
myself.

And while all that
was
happening.

While people
suffocated
and starved.

Terra chose
to save
animals, instead.

Is that right?
I don't know.

Is a human life
worth
more
than anything
else?

I already know
what my sister
would say.

The animals are worth it, Lee-Lee,
she'd whisper.

We can't let them
disappear.

THERE

From above,
The Ark looks
like a
buttery sea.

But as Henry
guides us
through
the air lock,

I see it's
something
more.

"Welcome to the
Savanna Platform,"
Henry says with a
grin.

"They're working on a
rainforest one.
But it's not
done."

"How do you know?"
asks Rose.

Grabbing his
arm.

"Careful, cuz!"
Henry laughs.

"You know
I'm steering the ship here,
right?"

"We're docked," groans Rose,
poking him.

Henry bats
her hand away.

"Well," says Henry.
"What can I say?

I'm a cab driver.
People talk."

Suddenly a voice
crackles
over the radio.

"Taxi 49. Urgent
pickup.

Drop what you're doing
and boogie.

You should have the
coordinates
now."

"Okay," says Henry,
squinting at a screen.

"Looks like there's
an important
transfer.

I’m going to drop
you two here.”

“When will you
be back?”
Rose asks.

Henry shrugs.

“Soon as I can, cuz.
Soon as I can.”

THE KISS

We climb down
the platform

and into a world
from
        the past.

Golden grasses
sweep
the horizon.

The liquid shadows
of shade trees
dot
    the land.

We're standing in
a fenced
        enclosure.

In the distance,
zebras
        graze.

Flamingos glow
pink as dawn.

"It's beautiful,"
I gasp.

Rose touches
my cheek.

Her hand
a whisper
on my
        skin.

When I feel her
gentle lips
on mine,

I know
I've found
something
            real.

THE ARK IS . . .

Flowers, elephants,
and exotic birds.

The feel of Rose's
skin
          on mine.

Our hands stay linked
when we leave
the
          enclosure.

And step into
this brilliant
          world.

EXPLORERS

"There could be lions,"
Rose whispers,
squeezing my hand.

But I don't sense
danger
        anywhere.

Instead, two giraffes
munch a palm's
                tender leaves.

Their calm, swaying bodies
prove we're
              safe.

Besides, all of my fear
has slipped away.

With Rose at my side,
her hand in mine.

I finally feel like
the real
        me.

WAITING

It's getting late,
and Henry isn't back.

We lie on our backs
inside The Ark's enclosure.

And stare up into
the dome.

"I'm so glad I found you,"
Rose whispers to me.

I laugh
as she traces her name
on my arm.

"Me too," I say,
trembling from the spark—

That electric current
of her skin
          on mine.

LOVING ROSE

I wonder if this is how
my sister feels?

Why she chose
Earth and Angus.

And gave Venus
to me.

When Rose says
my name,

my insides
shiver.

When our fingers
link,

my heart feels
whole.

Each cell in my body
wants to know her
                    completely.

When I hold her
against me,

I'm finally
free.

WHY I HATE LYING

I hate it
because
I care about
Rose.

And I want her
to know
everything.

After our visit
to The Ark,

we've grown so
close.

I ache to tell her
who I
am.

But when I wrote my
sister,

in our secret
code,

she answered,
"Don't you
dare."

POISON

I'm standing in a
strawberry field.

Trying to make sense of
a patch of
mold.

But my mind won't
focus.

I keep thinking of
Rose.

And what she told me
this morning.

About taking classes
on Acumen.

"Rachel," she'd said.

"Why not retake
the placement
exam?

You're so good
on Viridis.

You could
study botany
if your scores
go up."

I think of my sister,
the *real* Rachel.

If I retake the test,
could I be
found out?
I'm so lost
in my mind.

I don't hear
the plane.

A crop duster,
I realize.

But it's already
too
late.

Suddenly,
I'm coated
in white dust.

It's in my nose,
my mouth.

I can't
breathe!

That feeling of
drowning
rushes
back.

I reach for
my inhaler.

But it's not
there.

DYING

My eyes are on
fire.

My throat's
swelling shut.

My mind
is back

in our shack
          on Earth.

Rachel is
          outside.

My mother is
gripping
          my wrist.

"Promise,"
          she begs.

Her voice like
cracking
          ice.

"I can't have
both of my daughters
die.
Promise me, Leah.
Keep Rachel
               safe."

My lips say
the words.

But my heart
won't
agree.
If only I'd
listened,

Rachel would
be here
instead.
My superhero
sister.

Braver than
I'll ever
be.

Rachel,
the leader.

Who *always*
puts me first.

But instead of
Rachel,

it's me,
on the ground.

Thrashing in a field
of Venusian
strawberries.

Sobbing.

Dying.

Choking

for air.

RESCUE

I don't see them
coming.

I can't see
anything.

But I feel their
hands.

Hoisting me
up.

Their words—
"Get her to Sanitas
now!"

*The medical
platform?*
          I think.

Wanting to
          scream.

But when I try,
something stabs
into my
          arm.

"IV started,"
somebody shouts.

Then an
oxygen mask
is strapped
over my
        face.

I hear Flora's
voice.

It sounds like
she's
        sobbing.

"Why was she
out there?" shrieks Flora.

"Does anyone
                know?

Why didn't she
check
        the spray chart!"

A sharp wave
of fear
shoots
        through me.

I struggle
on the gurney.

I need to get
away.

The spray chart, I think.
It lists when
pesticides
        are dropped.

I was so busy thinking about
studying on
        Acumen,

I completely
forgot
        to check.

"Flora,"
        I groan.

But no one
understands.

Rachel,
I think.

We're about to get
caught.

TRANSPORT

I hear a
buzz.

Then feel
myself
rising.

The transport blimp
has
taken off.

My heart
lurches.

But I can
breathe better
now.

Maybe I can
stop them.

I don't want
to go.

"Wait!" I cry
through my oxygen
mask.

I twist
and turn.

Working to break
free.

A second needle
pricks
my arm.

"This should knock
her out,"
someone says.

Please!
I beg.

But only
in my mind.

Then the world
starts to
blur.

And
I'm
gone.

NIGHTMARE

In my dream,
I'm back on the
Egress.

Lieutenant Black's face
is in
mine.

"Liar!"
he snarls.
His spit
splatters
my skin.

"You know what
we have
to do!"

The scene
fades.
Now, I'm riding
in a
floating taxi.

Henry is
there.
And he looks
mad.

"Last ride, Lee-Lee,"
he sneers.

How does he
know
that name?

Now Rose is
beside him.

Her hair
like flames.

"How could you?"
she screams.
"I trusted you!"

The taxi's door
slides open.

And Captain Jarvis's voice
blares
over the intercom.

"You knew
what would happen
if you broke
the rules.
Now, you will
pay!"

Rose is
behind me.
She gives me a
shove.

"Stop!" I shriek
through a sea of
clouds.

But there's no
oxygen here.
And nowhere
to
run.

HOSPITAL

I hear:
"She's stable,"
as they rush me in.

My eyes are
so heavy.

Are they
weighted
        down?

Whatever they gave me
has started
wearing
        off.

But not enough
for me
        to move.

All I can do is
lie
    still.

Think my own
            thoughts.

And listen
            hard.

TWO NURSES THINKING I'M ASLEEP

"Dr. Elizabeth Breen
is going to
see her."

"Okay.
Well, when do you
think she'll
wake up?"

"They gave her a
heavy
sedative.
Could be
an hour.
Could be
less."

"Why does it have
to be Breen,
anyway?"

"Breen saw her at
intake,
back on
Earth.
She's the one
who ran
the qualifying tests."

"That makes sense.
But Elizabeth Breen . . .
Well, I shouldn't
                        say."

"You think she's
strange,
don't
          you?"

"I do.
I mean, she never
even got
          selected."

"Lots of folks
are born
          here."

"True.
But a friend of mine
works
in the archives
          on Acumen.
He says
Breen has a
          special pass.
Checks out
          whatever
          she wants.
Earth's ancient histories.
Political
          stuff.
Things we couldn't
get
   if we
          begged."

"Well, she must have
permission."

"I'm sure she does.
I just don't
trust her.
That's all.

You know,
She doesn't even
smile
when we pass.

Just looks right
through me.
Like I'm
air."

COMING BACK

It takes
a while.

But I start
coming back.

First I'm able to
open my
          eyes.

They sting a bit.
But I can see.

Luckily, whatever the medics
on Viridis
          gave me
made it so I could
breathe
          again.

I'm in a small,
white room.

Clean and
sterile

and filled with
fear.

An IV drips
something
into my
          arm.

Sanitas, I think.
What should I do?

But there's no time
to plan.

Before *she* steps
in.

The tall, blonde
woman.

With the hard
face.

"Hello there,"
says Dr. Breen.

"Rachel Silverton?"
She checks
my chart.

"How nice to see
you again."

Dr. Breen
doesn't
smile.

And I don't feel
nice.

All I feel
is
terrified.

OUT FOR BLOOD

"Well, Rachel," says
Dr. Breen.

Stepping closer to my
bed.

"Let me explain
what we're going
                    to do.

We've got your
breathing
under
          control.

The medics on Viridis
saved your life.

But I'd like to run
some tests
          before you go.

Just to be sure
you're
          okay."

"Tests?"
I croak.

I can't hide
the fear
boiling inside
                    me.

A secret volcano,
waiting
        to burst.

"Don't worry,"
says Dr. Breen.

"It's just a
basic
blood panel.

I also want
to scan
your lungs.

We'll probably
send you home
with an
        inhaler.

Have you ever
used one
        before?"

I feel like this woman,
with the
pale-blonde hair,

with the face that's
not pretty
because it's so
cold,

is trying
to make me
        confess.

"No," I lie,
praying she can't tell.

"Well, they're easy
to use,"
        says Dr. Breen.

"Not a big deal
                at all.

You really have
nothing
to worry about."

Her eyes
stare
into mine.

She doesn't
blink.

Not even
        once.

NO!

After Dr. Breen
leaves,

I don't know
what to
        do.

Part of me wants to
leap
from my bed.

Should I
try to hide?

Could I even
escape?

I keep thinking back
to Lieutenant Black's
words
on the *Egress.*

His careful
voice.

His awful
threat.

"Rachel," I whisper.
to my missing
                sister.

"I really wish
you
were here."

FINDING STRENGTH

Suddenly, a leaf
unfolds
inside my chest.

It's made of
blood.

And love.

And strength.

You have to fix this,
I think,

refusing to
cry.

No matter what,
you have to
find a
            way.

NOT SAFE

When the nurse
draws my blood,

I shut my
eyes.

I think of
Rachel
in our greenhouse
                    back home.

I see her
hugging Angus.

And looking
at me.

"We're safe,"
she'd said.

Well, not
         anymore.

"Don't worry, honey,"
says the nurse.

She has short,
gray hair
and
wrinkles
around her mouth.

I can tell she
probably
smiles
          a lot.

"We'll get you
out of here
soon.

When I'm finished,
someone from radiology
will take
you.

They'll do the chest
X-ray.

And then you'll be
done."

"Okay,"
I whisper.

My heart
a
drum.

"When will you get
my blood work
back?"

"Oh, by the end
of the night," she says.
"You'll already
be home
by then."

X-RAY

I hold my breath
when they take the
X-ray.

And try not to
think
about talking
to
          Rose.

How am I going
to tell her
          the truth?

For Rose,
a lie is like
a poisonous
          flower.

It's beauty
destroyed
once she knows
it can
          kill.

Like the oleander bush
outside
the Cibus Cafe.

(Rose wants to
rip it up.)

She prefers flowers
like
her namesake.

The kind you can
sprinkle
in salads.

Use to
decorate
cakes.

She sees no point
in the
toxic
kind.

Will she still see
the point
of me?

SAYING GOODBYE TO LIES

I sense her
before she
          enters.
Beautiful Rose,
with her fiery
                    hair.
A bolt of lightning
in my hospital room.

"Rachel, what happened?"
she asks,
starting to
             cry.

"I'm okay,"
I whisper.
But my throat
feels
    raw.

I peer into her
kind face.
Always so deep and smart
and calm.
My heart
hurts.

It's not from
love.
But from what
I have
          to do.

RESULTS

Before I can speak,
Dr. Breen walks in.

Rose is still
by my
          side.

And I'm still
deciding
what
          to say.

"Rachel," says
Dr. Breen.

Her blue eyes
hard.

"I reviewed your
X-ray.

And found something
strange.

Have you ever suffered from
asthma before?

Your scan shows
you
      have."

I make my face
blank.

But I can't stop
the fear.

Like a monster
inside me.

Clawing to
get out.

I shove my hands
beneath the
        hospital sheets.

So no one can see
that they're
starting
        to shake.

BAD NEWS

"Of course she doesn't
have asthma!"
Rose snaps.

"There must be
some
mistake."

"Scans don't lie," says
Dr. Breen.

"Well, you scanned her
back on Earth,"
argues Rose.
"She's the same person
now
that she was
then.
Whatever you saw
must have
happened in the
accident."

"I'm not so sure,"
says Dr. Breen.
"Rachel, I'm afraid you'll need
to stay
for more tests.

I can't let you
leave
until I know
what's
going
on."

Dr. Breen sighs and
scratches her head.

Then, a sliver of
sadness
slips behind her
eyes.

"Look, Rachel," she says.
"I'm not accusing you
of
anything.

I just need to
make sure
you're okay.

I wouldn't want you
having an attack
when you're
on your own."

Dr. Breen
blinks.

I don't
believe her.

I know she's trying to
keep me
calm,
while she works
things
out.

"An attack?"
repeats Rose,
taking my
hand.

"An asthma attack,"
says Dr. Breen.

"Well, can't you just
give her
medication
and send her
                    home?" asks Rose.
"It's not like
you won't know
where she
                is."

Dr. Breen
sighs.

I can tell by
her face
that she wants
to say
      yes.

In that moment, I remember
a conversation with Flora.

When we were
gardening
on Viridis.

Before all of
                    this.

CONVERSATION WITH FLORA

We're discussing
why Flora
chose not to
                    have kids.

And to be a
mentor
        instead.

I ask how many
others
decided that,
                    too.

"Many,"
Flora answers.

"And I think
you know
one of them.
Dr. Breen—
She did your
intake tests,
        right?"

I nod and wait for Flora
to go on.

"Well, she made the
same choice
        as me."

"You know," continues Flora,
wiping her brow,

"not only is Elizabeth Breen
Terra's
head medical screener.

But she's head of
genetic disease
prevention.
Dr. Breen screens
everyone
who wants to have
children."

"But isn't everyone
screened
before coming?"
I ask.

"Only the selected,"
says Flora.

"Those born here
aren't.
And it's
Dr. Breen
who makes the call.
If there's any sort of
genetic risk,
the answer is
always
no."

"Wow," I whisper.
"She must hate
telling people
that."

"It's part of
her job,"
Flora says.

"I've seen her
around
the different
platforms," says Flora.

"People say they
dislike her.
But I don't think
that's true.
I think
what they feel
is fear.
It's a hard life
she leads.

Putting what's best for
the city
before everything
else."

"But maybe she's wrong,"
I say.

"Maybe she should let
people do
what they
want."

"Maybe,"
says Flora.
"But either way,
she's a woman who stands
by her
beliefs.

Whatever anyone
thinks,
they can't doubt
that."

NEW INHALER

A nurse comes in
with an
inhaler.

Dr. Breen
takes it.

Then holds it
out
so I can
see.

"Okay, Rachel."
she says.
"Here's what
you do."

She shows me
where the cartridge
goes.

The right way
to inhale
the medication.

"Hold it in for
five seconds,"
instructs Dr. Breen.

I nod my
head.

Then do
what she asks.

While pretending
it's all
brand new.

I can't tell
if I've fooled her
or not.

All I know is that
Rose
is paying attention.

"In case you forget
anything," she says.

I try to
smile.

But inside
I feel
sick.

How can I tell Rose
the truth? I wonder.

How am I going to
let her
go?

BACK TO VIRIDIS

In the end,
Dr. Breen
lets us go.

I guess Rose's line
about how
there's nowhere to
hide

hits home
after all.

I mean,
we're not on
Earth.

I can't just
          disappear.

I'm trapped
in a world of
     clear, glass domes.

There's literally
no way to
          run.

HEADING HOME

Rose holds my hand
while we wait
for a
          taxi.

The streetlamps glow
like
fireflies.

Our domed world
softens in
          sleep.

It's almost 4 a.m.
when we arrive on
the Primis
               platform.

We head down
the leafy path
toward our building.

And I picture
my sister,
in a night of her
own.

I love you, Rose, I think.
squeezing her
hand.

And I hate what I'm
about to
          do.

BEFORE

"Are you okay?"
asks Rose.
We're in my room.
The world around us
dark and
still.

Such a small world,
I think.
Suddenly missing Earth.

That blue-green planet
so wild
and raw.

And so different
from where I am
right now.

I feel like
a bug
trapped beneath
glass.

Caught by a
child's
hand.

The child positions
the glass
so the sunlight
shines in.
Revealing my
secrets.
Making me
burn.

GETTING READY

"Rose,"
I whisper.
"There's something
I need
          to say."

I take a pull from
my inhaler.

Expertly lifting it
to my
          lips.

One, two, three, four, five,
I count.

Okay,
I think.

Time to
          talk.

SAYING IT

"My name isn't
Rachel."

My voice sounds
small.

Like I've turned
into
          a kid again.

"Rachel's my
sister.

She looks
just like
          me.

Only nothing's actually
wrong
with her."

"What do you mean?" asks
Rose.

Her tone is
          sharp.

She takes
a step back.

Toward the
door.

"My name is Leah,"
I whisper.

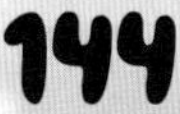

"Leah
Silverton.

That damage Dr. Breen saw
on my X-ray . . .

Well, it wasn't
just
from today.

It's old scarring
from
pollution-induced asthma.

The kind
that killed my parents.
That would have
killed
me, too.

If my sister,
Rachel,
hadn't given me her spot.

So I could board
the *Egress*.
And
survive.

I didn't even
ask her.
She decided
on her own.

I guess the only
way
to save me

was for her
to pretend
to *be* me.

But now the trick
is up.

Dr. Breen
          knows.

Or at least she will once
she checks
my blood type.

Rachel's type O.
And I'm
          type A.

There's no way I can
lie
my way
          out of that."

I pause
for a moment.

I stare into
the night.

From my window,
I make out
the oleander bush
Rose
          hates.

Its pale flowers
hiding
the poison
                    within.

AFTER

Rose's eyes
are
two moons.

At first,
she's silent.

Then she starts
to cry.

"Rose," I reach
for her.

She backs
away.

"Liar!"
she hisses.

"You lied
about everything!"

"I'm sorry,"
I say.

My hands
are shaking
again.

And then
it comes.

That terrible
feeling.

Like all the
oxygen
has been sucked
from the room.

And my lungs
are
two clenched fists.

"Your medication!"
Rose cries.

I grab
my inhaler.

Take a pull,
and count
            to five.

WAITING

Rose sits on
my bed
for a very long
time.

The streetlamps
shimmer
on the paths
below.

Viridis's plants
stretch toward the
domed roof.

While my heart
waits.

For what Rose
has to
say.

ROSE'S DECISION

"I love you,"
says Rose.

Finally looking
at me.

Tears stream
down
her face.

But she
ignores them.

And takes
my hand.

Then folds me
softly
into her arms.

"But I hate
that you lied,"
she whispers.

Her words
burn
my skin.

"To me.
To Flora.
To everyone.

Except, I know why
your sister
did what she
did.

You see,"
says Rose,

"I have
a secret, too.

My little brother
had terrible
asthma.

When he died,
I decided
I wouldn't
come here.

I wasn't even going to
take
the exams.

But my mother
drugged me.

And took me to
the testing site.

When I was
selected,
she made me
go.

At first,
I was angry.

I thought she was
pushing
me away.

But that wasn't really
it
at all.

My mom
needed
to save me.

Just like your sister
had to save you.

I guess,
sometimes,
when you really
love
somebody,

it's okay
to break
the
rules."

ESCAPE

We rush
from the dorm.
Avoiding the
elevator.
Rose makes us
take
the stairs
instead.

(She says it's
less likely
we'll see someone
that way.)

But our footsteps
ring
as loud as
gunshots.
As loud as
my heartbeat—

blaring in
my ears.

Outside,
the dome is
still set
to night.
But soon our world
will be light
again.
And then they'll come
searching.

I know
they will.

I just have to pray
Rose has
a good place to
hide.

MY FACE

We peel out
of the building.

My breath is so
ragged,

it's hard
to breathe.

I take a
drag
from my
          inhaler.

Then glance
into the
          quiet dark.

"Rose!"
I cry.

Because there it
is.

My face, on
the TV screen.

The huge one
          that hangs

in the gardens of
Primis.

I pull out
my cell.

It's on there,
too.

"No!"
cries Rose.

Not believing
what
        she sees.

Red letters march
across
the bottom
        of my cell phone.

I see the word
"criminal."

And
"wanted for
        arrest."

"GIVE ME YOUR CELL PHONE!"

Rose says.

"They can
track it!"

She tosses it
into
the oleander
bush.

Along with
her own.

I watch them
slip beneath
the toxic
blossoms.

Lost in the
leafy green
below.

MANHOLE

"Okay," pants Rose.
"Now, let's go."
She grabs my
hand.
And drags me down
the path.

At first, I think
we're heading
to the
          Cibus Cafe.

But before
we get there,
Rose makes a
hard
          left.

Then she's
off the path.
On her knees,
                    digging.

Her fingers raking
at the earth.
"Help me!"
she cries.

And then I see it.
The silver glint
of the manhole
cover.

Buried in the
undergrowth.

INSIDE

We're beneath the
Primis platform.

Far below
the transparent
dome.

We huddle
together.

In a long, dark
hallway.

Ribbed in
piping

and metal
grates.

It's so narrow
down
here.

We can't even
stand.

And it smells like
must and
decay.

I peer
into
the darkness.

Eyes
          straining.

Scared of what
might be

lurking
down here.

Maybe something
that thinks

we'd make a nice
snack?

Get it together,
I think.

And force
my fear
          down.

Then Rose
grabs my arm.

And I can
breathe
          again.

"Listen," says Rose,
pointing down.

I close
          my eyes.

Narrow
my senses.

And that's when
I hear it.

Far
below.

The quiet hum
of the platform's
propellers.

Keeping us
always
trapped in
light.

ROSE'S PHONE

Rose pulls
a cell phone

from her
pocket.

"Hey,"
I whisper.

"I thought they could
track us
with those."

"This one's
untraceable,"
she says.

"It's completely
off the
grid."

Then she
glares.

"Rose?"
I say.

She shakes her head.
Hard.

As if wiping away
an unwanted
thought.

"Sorry, Rachel . . .
I mean Leah," she says.

Rose runs
a hand
through her
hair.

Now a tangled,
matted mess.

"I guess I'm
still mad."

She touches my
cheek.

"I don't want to be.
But I
        am.

I'm not sorry
I'm doing this,
                    though."

She
    sighs.

"I'm going to text
Henry now.

He's the one who
gave me
the phone.

Just in case
things
ever went bad.

That's Henry
for you.

Always thinking through
every
angle.

Anyway, he'll know
what we
should do.

Or at the
very least,

he'll have
a better place
to hide."

WHAT HENRY SAYS

He says to
wait
until
        midnight.

When our world's
completely
asleep.

Then
meet him

at the taxi
stand.

He'll be there.
Ready to
        help.

For now,
we have to
sit tight.

Making certain
we're not
        seen.

STAYING PUT

It's day
        again.

Bright shafts
of light

slip through
the cracks
        above.

Rose and I
            sit.

Backs pressed against
each other.

Counting the hours
until it's
         time.

My stomach
rumbles.

Rose's does,
too.

Alerting us
time
is moving on.

I ache to
make a joke.

Or tell her
I love her.

Or apologize
for all the
          lies.

But the words stay
trapped
inside my mind.

And instead, I just
focus
on my
          breathing.

And what it is
we're about
                    to do.

ROSE SPEAKS

"Why did you
do it?"
whispers
        Rose.

Her back is still
pressed
against
        mine.

I can feel her
breathing.

Her warmth hopeful
as the
        sun.

And I know
exactly
what she means.

Not why did I lie
my way
        to Venus.

But why did I
lie
to her.

MY RESPONSE

"I'm sorry,"
I whisper.

My voice is a
blade.

Slicing into the person
I love
the most.

"I didn't mean for this
to happen," I say.

"I didn't want to
fall for
you.

My plan was to
stay single.

To not
make
any friends.

That way,
I wouldn't have to
lie
so much.

And it would be
easier
to pretend to be
somebody else.

But then,
I met
you.

That very first
day.

I even asked
my sister
what I should
do.
I wanted to
tell you.

But she said
no.

That it'd be
too risky.

And I thought
she was
right.

But I guess
my lying

didn't change
anything.

Because you're
still
in this mess, too."

My heart
flutters
as I speak.

My breath
goes short.

Rose
hands me
my inhaler.

Then squeezes
my arm.

As if to say
it's all right.

Even though I know
it's not.

TIME TO RUN

It's midnight
and the

shafts of light
in the ceiling

disappeared
hours ago.

"Time to run,"
whispers Rose.

Her words are
sharp
in my ear.

I swallow
hard.

And say,
"Let's go."

DEAD OR ALIVE

We stumble out of
the manhole.
And into
the night.

In the shadows,
we jog
toward the taxi
stand.

I can tell
right away—
something's
wrong.

I see guards at
the elevator.
Guns in their
hands.

Then I hear
the voice
from my dreams.

Dark and bitter.
Hunting
me down.

"Find them!" barks
Lieutenant Black.

"I don't care
if we take them
dead
or
alive."

WHAT I KNOW ABOUT LIEUTENANT BLACK

He was
born on Earth.

To a poor
family.

Too poor to spend money
on
        internet cafes.

They say sometimes,
when he thinks
nobody's
        looking,

he pulls out a
worn
        family photo
                and cries.

That must mean
his heart's

not as cold
as his name.

Though most say
he's
completely
        heartless.

Willing to do
anything

to move up
the ranks.

That's why I fear
his
shark-gray eyes.

Waiting for me
to make a
mistake.

HENRY'S BLIMP

"Where is it?"
Rose hisses.

Jolting me
from
my thoughts.

We've been standing
frozen
in the darkness.

Close enough to see
the taxi stand.

And Henry, well . . .
he isn't
          here.

EXPLOSION

The world
vibrates

with a
          terrible
               crack.

Black is
howling orders.

Then the guards
disappear.

Leaving us
          all alone.

"GO!"

shrieks
        Rose.

We rush
into
        the elevator.

Gripping hands
as it
    goes
        up.

Below us
flashes

a sea of
        lanterns.

In the distance,
people
        scream.

HENRY!

We step out of
the elevator.

There's a ladder,
dangling
from the sky.

I look up
and
Henry
waves.

"You first,"
Rose insists.

I don't
argue.

All I do is
start
to climb.

The darkness
swallows me
like a secret.

I move toward
safety
in the
sky.

WHAT HENRY DID

"How'd you do it?"
Rose asks.

She stares
at Henry

as he guides
the blimp

through the
clouds.

"Explosives,"
he answers.

"Got them
through a
connection."

"Henry,"
says Rose.

"That was
too much of a
risk!"

"Not for family,"
he replies.

"Besides,
the atmospheric pressure
is the same
inside *and* outside
the dome.

All I did
was make an
air leak.

They'll have it
patched
fast."

"We better hope so,"
says Rose,
glancing at me.

"Now, where can we go
that's safe?"

HENRY'S PLAN

"Remember that rainforest
platform?"
says Henry.

We're flying toward the
city's
rim.

The radio's on,
so we can hear
what happened.

Henry was
right.

They're fixing
the crack.

Soon they'll be
searching
for us
again.

"Henry," I whisper,
realizing what this
means.

"They're going to know
you helped us.

What are you
going
to do?"

"Don't worry,"
he says.

"My explosives contact
won't talk.

It'll take Black a while
to figure it out.

It's you
I'm concerned
about.

The rainforest platform
is pretty remote.

The scientists
want it to
grow
on its own.

Sort of like
what happens
on Earth.

Someone checks on it
now and then.

But if you
stay hidden,

you'll be
safe.

Just find shelter and
water.

I know
it's there.

Then wait for everyone to
forget you.

Something new will
come up.

It always
does.

Captain Jarvis will
probably
write you off
as dead."

"But what about
my sister?" I say.

"She needs to
know
what's going on."

TELLING RACHEL

In the end,
Henry lets me
send
          one text.

And only after
he learns

I'm writing
in code.

"Use the phone
I gave Rose," he says.

"Then, that's it.
No more messages.

And keep it
turned off.

At least for
a while."

GOODBYES

There's no
glass elevator
here.

Just a high,
concrete tower.
A metal ladder
instead
of stairs.

Henry hugs Rose
goodbye.
Then hugs
me, too.

"Take care of her,"
he whispers
in my ear.

"I will," I say,
giving him
a squeeze.

Then he climbs aboard
his blimp.

He waves.
Then he is gone.

And all that is left
is a sea
of green.

And an emptiness
inside
my heart.

MESSAGE TO RACHEL

They know.

Find safety.

I'm okay.

NEW LIFE

This world of
green

is something
new.

Luckily, Rose and I
know

some plants
to eat.

(All that gardening in Viridis
really paid off.)

And there's always
fish

and birds,
too.

We built a shelter
in the trees.

Safe from
the predators
that roam
this place.

And well
hidden.

Though, so far,
we haven't seen
anyone.

Our phone is
solar.

So it stays
charged.

I check it
once
every week.

But it doesn't even
pick up
Terra's general
messages.

(The ones they
cast on the TVs
in Primis.)

I guess being untraceable
means
we can't see
news.

FOUR MONTHS PASS

Then Rachel's message
comes through.
"I'm safe," it says
in our special
code.
"Angus, Henry, and I
are in the
mountains.
Stay strong,
I'll see you
someday
soon."

My heart
blooms.

When I tell Rose,
she smiles.
Relieved to hear
Henry's
okay.

Even though this means
he was
definitely
caught.

Even though it means
we're on
our own.

"NOT YET"

Rose says
when I ask

if she thinks
we've been
forgotten.

Her green eyes
glow
in this leafy
world.

Full of the wild
I've grown
to love.

EARLY ONE MORNING

I think of
my sister.

And how she
always
fought to save me.

Making sure
I survived.

My asthma's
improved.

I don't need my inhaler
anymore.

I have her to thank
for everything.

I close my
eyes.
And imagine
her presence.

Knowing,
even though she's on
another
planet,

our hearts still
beat
beneath the same
bright
sun.

WANT TO KEEP READING?

If you liked this book, check out another book from West 44 Books:

THE LAST STAR CHASER

BY DEMITRIA LUNETTA

ISBN: 9781978597129

My (clueless) parents
thought this (space) cruise
would be the perfect (family) vacation.

It's one of the first (luxury cruise) spaceships
(my dad gushes) and my mom
thinks it will be good for us (as a family).

It's the last of its kind (my mom says).
What I hear is that it's old (and outdated).
And should be broken down (for parts).

My abnormal (eight-year-old) brother
Kain (the pain) is all about it.
He's obsessed with space (the total astro-geek).

Kain with his (floppy) brown hair
and (big) brown eyes
and (goofy) smile.

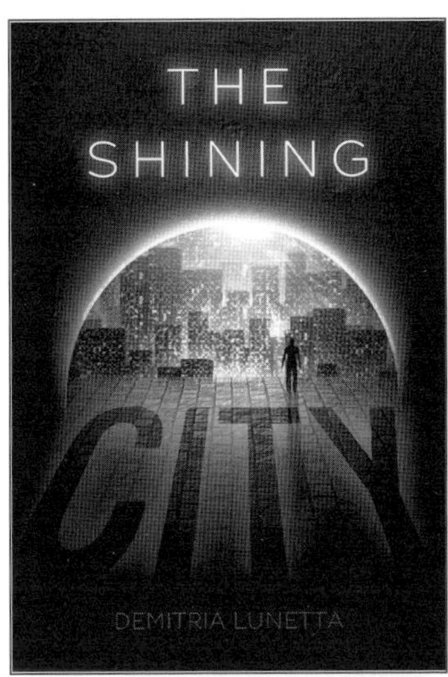
THE
SHINING
CITY
DEMITRIA LUNETTA

Take a
Sad Song
Ona Gritz
STEREO
45

OUR
BROKEN
EARTH
DEMITRIA LUNETTA

THE BRUJOS OF
BORDERLAND
HIGH
GUME LAUREL III

ABOUT THE AUTHOR

Maija Barnett grew up in central Vermont and now lives in Massachusetts with her husband and two teenage daughters. She loves nature, poetry, hiking in the woods with her dogs, and finding ways to get kids excited about reading. Maija holds degrees in English and teaching and currently teaches at a school for students with learning differences. *Reaching for Venus* is her third novel.